"A fire glow in the distance,
and then the wavy line
of burning grass,
gave notice
that the Indians
were in the Valley
clearing ground …
to obtain
their winter supply
of acorns
and wild
sweet potato root
(huckhau)."

- H. Willis Baxley, 1861

Ponderosa Pine
by Emily Underwood

Who Needs a Forest Fire? was commissioned by Nevada County Arts Council for FOREST ⇌ FIRE, as presented to the people of the Truckee-Tahoe region of California. The book was created specifically for FOREST ⇌ FIRE in collaboration with the project creators Llewellyn Studio and was made possible through the generous support of the Tahoe Truckee Excellence in Education Foundation and the California Arts Council's Creative California Community grant program. Educational and environmental outreach with Sierra Watershed Education Partnerships.

FOREST ⇌ FIRE

www.forestandfire.org

Designed by Carolyn Bennett Fraiser, www.carolynbfraiser.com

Copyright © 2021 Terra Bella Books
Library of Congress Control Number: 2021901594
ISBN: (print edition) 978-1-7357212-0-0
(e-book edition) 978-1-7357212-1-7

Independently published by:

www.TerraBellaBooks.com
Los Angeles, California

Author's Note

Some of the details in this book may not be true for every Native American tribe in California and Nevada. Although this book refers to the Sierra Nevada area, it is not the only region that has been affected by forest fires.

California has been, and still is, home to these tribes and their culture. Tribal people continue to tend to their age-old plant gathering and plant management traditions.

Terminology

The terms 'Indigenous', 'Native American' and 'American Indian' refer to the people who first lived in this part of the United States, as well as everyone related to those first people.

Who Needs A Forest Fire?

Paula Henson

illustrated by **Sue Todd**

and Emily Underwood

Terra Bella Books
Los Angeles, California

Who Came First?

THE HUMANS OR THE TREES?

It was the end of an ice age. The first humans appeared in the Sierra Nevada Mountains about 13,000 years ago. The first **saplings** grew around the same time.

The people and the trees needed each other to survive. The forest needed to be cared for, especially the forest floor.

Does the Forest Need Fire?

Some forests do need fire. It is part of the natural cycle. Without it, young trees grow too close together, blocking the sun. Dry, dead leaves, pine needles and branches collect too deeply on the forest floor.

Native Americans do not fight fire. Fire is not an enemy. To Native American people, each part of nature is a living being. All parts have a spirit. The forest is like a family. If just one member of the family is sick, everyone suffers.

To help keep the forests healthy, they use fire.

Black Oak

Who Needs Fire?

PLANTS DO!

Plants cannot run, fly, creep, or crawl away from fire. Plant roots are often protected underground, away from the fire. When a plant burns, the root system releases **nutrients** and the plant re-sprouts. Even though fire destroys things, it also brings new life.

Soap Plant

Ponderosa Pine Cone

Who Else Needs Fire?

ANIMALS DO!

A forest full of burned trees is not a place you would want to live but many animals and insects cannot wait to move in! Animals don't like fire, but it keeps their habitats healthy.

Fire clears out meadows for **grazing** animals. Birds and small animals use **snags** to hide from **predators**. Squirrels, chipmunks, wood rats, and other small mammals will come back when there is food to eat.

Lewis' Woodpecker

Fire Beetle

Pronghorn Antelope

Illustrations by Emily Underwood

And Who Else Needs Fire?

HUMANS DO!

Native American people used small fires as a tool. It kept the forests healthy. Healthy forests with large trees and big open spaces help provide clear air and water, which all humans need. Some areas of forest are still maintained this way.

These fires would renew the plants people needed for supplies like toys, baskets, feather skirts, strings for hunting bows, and even earplugs!

Plants also supply medicine. California poppies help toothaches. Tobacco was used to help heal cuts. Pine nuts can be used to treat spider bites, and willow bark is a treatment for fevers.

But things changed, and the forests would never be the same.

How Did Forests Change?

Our relationship with fire changed with the Gold Rush. Newly arrived explorers, settlers and miners thought they should **clear-cut** all of the large trees to build things like railroads and mines. They thought selling the **timber** was a good idea. They didn't understand that by taking too much, it hurt the forest.

They tried to control nature, not care for it. No fires could be set and all fires had to be immediately **extinguished**. No trees should be wasted. They couldn't understand why the Native American people were setting fires that could possibly destroy the timber.

Why Are There Megafires Now?

After the Gold Rush most of the forest was no longer cared for. Saplings grew in crowded masses. Many plants died because the sunlight was blocked. **Duff** built up on the forest floor preventing rain from getting to the soil.

This created the perfect conditions for major wildfires called **megafires**.

Climate change is also making it harder to stop massive fires. Without any water, many trees and plants are unhealthy and easily catch fire. Dry brush can be hit by lightning strikes and start a new blaze. Sparks, **embers** and smoke blow in all directions.

Does the Forest Still Need People?

We still need each other. It seems odd but the forest need fires more often, just not megafires. Using controlled burns, there will be less fuel, smaller fires will cause less damage and will not last as long.

We must rebuild our partnership with the forest. All living things can continue to live in a healthy environment if we use the best ways for tending our forests. Taking care of the forest **ecosystem** correctly can reduce the number of wildfires and megafires.

Today we have different needs than the first humans did. We still need things like oxygen to breathe and clean water to drink.

Thank you, trees, for the clean air!

Thank you for clean water!

What does the forest need from us?

- The forest floor needs to be cared for.

- It needs to be restored.

- It needs to be resilient to recover from human disruptions

- It needs biodiversity so living things have healthier **habitats**.

What Can People Do?

It's a very big job to make sure 33 million acres of trees don't burn down. Fires are unpredictable, fast and powerful. Sometimes the only safe way to deal with fires is to stay out of the way!

We will always need firefighters for safety but we must understand the wisdom of the Native American people. This tribal knowledge is part of rebuilding **ecosystems** and becoming **resilient** as fires continue.

Work is already being done to learn from the indigenous peoples who know the forest well. Fire scientists, foresters and other experts now use methods like **prescribed fires**.

Once our forests are healthy, **traditional** or **cultural burning** can be used to restore a forest's **biodiversity** and keep it safe from megafires.

Students plant native Sugar pine trees as part of SWEP's Forest Health Field Program. Photo credit: SWEP Staff

Find Out More

The following pages include information on:

FIRE

- *What is Fire?*
- *Types of Fire*
- *Two Ways to Manage a Forest*
- *How Can People Plan for Fire?*
- *How Can Wildfires be Stopped?*
- *What to do if there is a Wildfire in Your Area*
- *What About Smoke?*

NATIVE AMERICANS

- *How do Native Americans Start a Traditional Fire?*
- *The Washoe and Miwok Tribes*
- *Native American Food*
- *Acorns*

CALIFORNIA

- *Native Plants*
- *Fire-Adapted Plants*
- *Native Animals*
- *Fire-Adapted Animals*

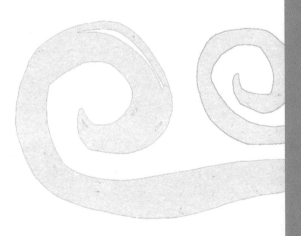

Questions to Consider

Why do humans get to decide what happens to the trees?

Should people be allowed to build homes in areas in danger of wildfire?

Are there ways to help protect animals from megafires?

Imagine you are in a forest. What do you see/hear/feel/ smell?

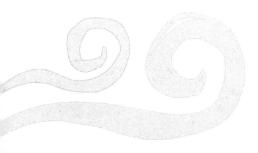

FIRE:
What is Fire ?

Fire is a chemical reaction. It releases light and heat. Combustion is a reaction between oxygen and fuel. Flames are the part of a fire that we can see, and it can be different colors depending on what is burning.

The three things needed for fire are called the **Fire Triangle**.

1. **Oxygen** — Air or wind

2. **Heat** — The ignition (or start)

3. **Fuel** — Plants including trees and grasses, or homes

Think about the ingredients you need to build a fire in your fireplace at home. It only takes dry logs, some **kindling** (like pine needles), and **ignition**, like a match. Without any one of these things you won't have a fire. It's the same thing with a wildfire. Make sure there are no dangerous fire ingredients around your home!

Humans learned to control fire about 400,000 years ago.

We are the only species that can ignite it, maintain it, and spread it where we want it to go.

Types of Fire

Wildfires

Wildfires are not planned or even known about until someone notices the smoke. People can be careless about cigarettes, unattended campfires, or fireworks.

In an uncared for forest with dense duff and dry trees, under certain conditions (wind), wildfires can become **megafires**. In a well cared for forest, far away from where people live, wildfires can be left to burn. They won't get too hot or hurt the forest.

Cultural or Traditional fires

Native Americans learned from watching wildfires. They traditionally set small fires to burn and clear the forest floor. Small, planned fires don't move very fast and only last a short time. It is a pretty safe way to get rid of **duff** and **invasive** or diseased plants.

Controlled or Prescribed fires

Fire experts plan ways to only burn specific areas of the forest that need clearing. Plenty of safety measures are in place and they only set the fires if the conditions are just right (no wind).

Megafires and Gigafires

Wildfires that become megafires gain strength from the wind that they create. These fires harm the forest and are very dangerous for people. Megafires that burn over a million acres are called gigafires. They can be impossible to put out. But if they can be contained to specific areas, they can do less damage.

Megafires and gigafires can become so hot that roots die. The **scorched** soil cannot absorb rain. When rain falls, it washes soil and ashes into streams, **polluting** them.

Two Ways to Manage a Forest

Images on the left side (view top to bottom) show a forest without good management. The trees are too dense, the fires are larger, burn up to the tops of the trees and then there are no trees left.

Images on the right side, (view from top to bottom) **ecological thinning** keeps the forest from getting too dense, the fires stay on the ground and many large trees survive.

Art by Emily Underwood

How Can People Plan for Fire

1. Make sure everyone in your family or group knows your **safety plan**

2. Practice **evacuations**.

3. Create a defensible space around your home that is kept clear of anything that could burn.

4. **Ecological thinning** removes small trees and **brush** that burn easily. Fires can climb up dead branches to the tree canopy and then to other trees.

5. **Grazing** animals can help. On grasslands and some steep hillsides livestock such as cattle, sheep, goats and horses can eat the fuel. The type of vegetation determines which animal is best but goats will eat almost anything!

6. Find Your 5 (http://www.mynevadacounty.com/2760/Find-Your-Five-Share-Your-Plan). Use this website to prepare for an emergency! Be ready with a list of contacts, evacuation routes, a meeting place and a list of essential items.

Goats chew through grass on a hill to keep wildfire risk down. Stock image.

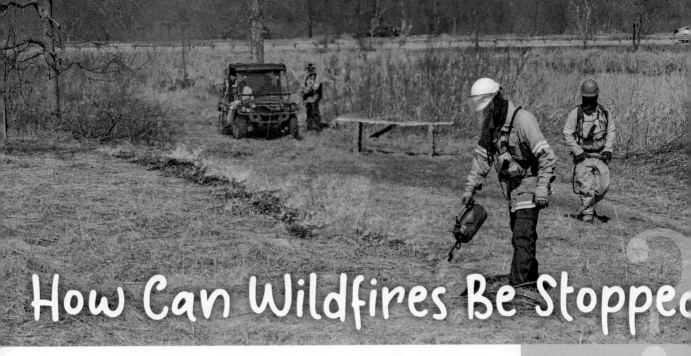

How Can Wildfires Be Stoppec

CAL FIRE (The California Department of Forestry and Fire Protection) (www.fire.ca.gov) is the state fire agency. They work together with other fire agencies like the U.S. Forest Service, local crews, and other emergency services. CAL FIRE also responds to other urgent situations like structure fires, floods, hazardous materials spills, swift water rescues, earthquakes, and all kinds of medical emergencies.

Many fires are unexpected. If a dead or dry tree is hit by lightning, it can burst into flames. A gust of wind might quickly send the flames in a different direction. People and animals scurry to find shelter and birds take flight to escape.

Professional firefighters have many ways to handle a fire. In a forest it may be hard to find a water source so they use **retardants** to stop the flames. Special planes can drop thousands of gallons of water from above.

Firebreaks, **fire lines** and **backfires** are planned ahead of the flames. The idea is to remove (or "pre" burn) everything in the path of the fire, so there is nothing left to burn. Special crews are trained to predict where the fire may go.

Fires can be stopped in 3 different ways:

1. Taking away the **fuel** source.

2. Taking away the oxygen by **tamping** it down.

3. Taking away the heat by spraying it with water.

What To Do If There Is A Fire In Your Area

1. Evacuate as soon as possible. Don't wait.

2. When you are somewhere safe, contact 9-1-1 or a local fire department or park service.

3. If possible, have a moist cloth or mask to reduce smoke **inhalation**.

4. Never leave a fire unattended. If you have a campfire, make sure it is completely **extinguished**.

5. Use shovels, axes and other tools to help control a fire and **tamp** it down.

6. Follow rules about burning things in your area, especially if it is windy.

What about Smoke

The first sign of a fire is usually silent, and seen from a distance. It's also the last sign of a fire. Smoke can hang in the air for days or even weeks after a fire. The reddish, hazy air can stay in an area, especially when winds die down. It causes stinging eyes, coughing, and you can't escape the smell in your clothes.

What is smoke? It's a mixture of tiny **particles**, gases and even **water vapor**. Because smoke rises (sometimes it can be 14 miles up), it can also travel a long way. Forest fire smoke from California wildfires has blown as far as New York - nearly 2,500 miles - and can even be seen from the International Space Station!

In ancient times there were fires burning all the time during the summer months as part of the natural processes of the forest. Smoke is part of that natural process. It drives away insects and **parasites**, which attack some shrubs and trees. It reflects sunlight, keeping river water cool for salmon.

Native Americans

To the Native American people, each part of nature (plants, animals, people, water, air, soil and fire) is a living being. All parts have a spirit (even rocks). The forest is like a family.

When the Native Americans tended the forest, new saplings were only allowed to grow in specific areas of the forest, leaving open, sunny areas that were not dense with trees.

Several California tribes are known for making baskets. Just one basket uses over 600 tree **shoots**, 3,000 wildflower stalks and 1,000 grass stalks! When they need more baskets, the Native Americans can burn more **vegetation**, and then wait for the new **shoots** to grow.

The Native American culture still exists. There are 109 official tribes in California today but there were over 500. Most have their own customs, clothing, crafts, food and even language. Many tribal members live on **reservations**.

Some California Tribes

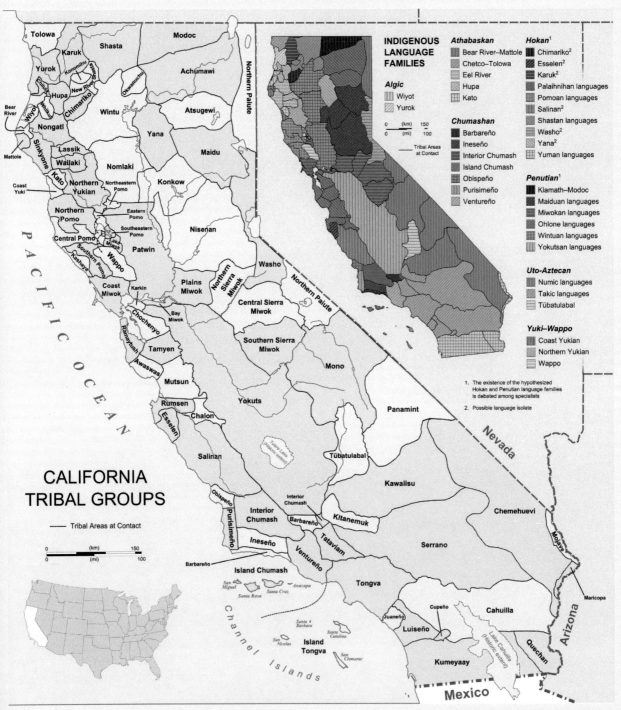

Concerto (https://commons.wikimedia.org/wiki/File:California_tribes_&_languages_
at_contact.png), „California tribes & languages at contact", https://creativecommons.
org/licenses/by-sa/3.0/legalcode

Holes in these rocks were used by Washoe people for grinding acorns, pine nuts and other nuts.
Stock Image.

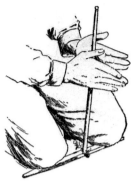

California's forest fires affect many people. The Washoe and Miwok are two tribes that lived in the area until the Gold Rush in the 1840s. As other people arrived, the wildfires became more common and destructive. The people of all tribes suffered, not just the ones that lived in the Sierra Nevada area.

The name Washoe (or Washo) comes from the word **Wa:šiw** meaning people from here. The Washoe are famous for basketweaving. The tribe members would move as the seasons changed. Today there are about 1,500 members of the tribe in Nevada and California.

The Miwok is another tribe from the Sierra Nevada area. The Chaw-se Indian Grinding Rock is in a Miwok village where bedrock is still used to grind acorns. Buildings called cha'kas stored the acorns. They were lined with pine needles and wormwood to keep away insects and rodents. Tree branches on top keep out rain and snow.

How do Native Americans start a traditional fire?

1. Percussion is striking two objects like stones together to create a spark.

2. A torch (also called a 'slow match') is made of heron, hawk, or buzzard tail feathers.

3. Drilling creates heat from the friction of rotating a stick in a hole in a bore.

Black Morel mushrooms
(Stock Image)

Elderberries —These were used to prevent the flu

Hazelnut (also called filbert) — It has a thick shell and is now mostly grown in Oregon.

Huckhau — It's also called Wild Sweet Potato root.

Yampah —This tuber is like a wild carrot or potato.

Manzanita —The berries are ground into flour, and used for cider, sauce, or soup.

Native American Food

The first Native Americans got food from plants and animals. They ate seeds, nuts, berries, tubers and roots. But they also ate fish, deer, rabbits and game birds. Some animals were not hunted, killed or eaten—they were considered **sacred**.

Elderberries (Stock Image)

Pine nuts — They could be roasted then pounded into flour. They could also be made into soup.

Black Morel Mushroom — A hollow fungus that must be cooked before it's eaten.

Manzanita berries (Stock Image)

Acorns

Preparing acorns to eat is not so easy. You cannot just pick and eat an acorn.

Acorns **MUST** be **leached** because raw acorns are poisonous for humans!

Acorns *(Stock Image)*

First they were sprinkled with water to loosen their outer shell. Then they were dried in the sun then pounded into flour…then **leached**… then made into soup, mush or biscuits. The black oak or tan oak acorns have the most flavor.

Fire-adapted Plants

Lodgepole Pine — The **resin** in the cone melts, the **scales** open, and seeds are released.

Ponderosa Pine — Its thick bark helps it survive a small fire. As it grows, it drops its lower branches, which prevents fire from climbing up and burning its tree top.

Black Morel Mushrooms — They are a **fungus**. They wait underground until moisture and nutrients have returned to the soil after a fire.

Hazelnut bushes — After the tree burns, new **shoots** come up and people used them for making snowshoes, arrows, rope, and baskets.

Hazelnuts *(Stock Image)*

Native Plants

Non-native plants are sometime invasive. They will "take over" areas crowding out the natives. Traditional or prescribed burns can get rid of invasive plants.

Soap Plant, Amole, or wavyleaf soap plant is a bulb that was used for other things besides soap. The fibers from the bulbs were used as brushes. Mashed bulbs could be used for glue on arrow feathers.

Sugar Pine is the largest pine in the world and they have the longest cones. Its resin is sweet.

Jeffrey and Ponderosa Pines are hard to tell apart except the bark of the Jeffrey pine is said to smell of butterscotch and vanilla! The Ponderosa pine has no scent. The sap of these types of pines was used to make candy, baskets and medicine.

Manzanitas have small white or pink flowers and brownish-red fruits that look like tiny apples (manzanita means 'little apple' in Spanish).

Poppies are the native California state flower. If you find a dried poppy seed pod it might "pop" open and spread its seeds.

Poppies (Stock Image)

Homes for Old Trees

A path through an old-growth forest (Stock Image)

An **old-growth forest** is not only a home for large, elderly trees. Trees can be a source of food. They are not grown because they are pretty. But people living in the forests needed to be able to see each other through the trees. A clear view of animals from a distance made hunting easier.

Old-growth forests hold large amounts of **carbon** in their wood, which helps the environment. One of the oldest living things on earth are the Bristlecone pines. Some growing in California are almost 5,000 years old.

Big trees with thick bark can survive wildfire, so some forests become places with very large trees and big open spaces. This makes room for sunny meadows and new life. There will be some trees that survive the blaze and will show **fire scar**s for years.

Practical Plant Parts

Oaks give us acorns — Native Americans call oaks 'Acorn Trees'. Acorn soup and acorn bread are common foods.

Pines give us pinecones — Besides the delicious pine nuts, pines were traditionally used to make toys, jewelry, and bows.

Amole gives us…soap? Juice from the California soaproot or Soap Lily plant is used for making soap.

Native Animals

All sorts of animals are native to the Sierra Nevada area of California and there are lots of wanderers too. Native chipmunks, quail, salmon, hermit thrushes, and the red-capped acorn woodpecker live here but also hummingbirds and western tanagers that are not native.

Mule deer – They are deer, but with mule-like ears!

California newt – It lives only in California and this salamander is toxic. Don't pick one up and definitely don't eat one!

Pronghorn antelope – One of the fastest land mammals in North America. It is related to goats, and looks like a deer, but is actually not an antelope.

California Newt (Stock Image)

Tule Elk – They used to live in large herds of 1,000 to 3,000.

Mule Deer (Stock Image)

Fire-adapted Animals

Black Backed Woodpeckers use both large and small dead trees for nesting and foraging. They make holes that are later used by **cavity**-nesting birds.

Spotted Owls nest and **roost** in lightly burned large trees.

Lewis's woodpecker – Oddly, this bird rarely pecks at wood.

More Questions

What surprised you in this book?

What does the author want you to learn from this book?

Should people be able to take what they want from the forest?

Can you think of any other words to describe a fire?

Who should decide things like who owns the trees in the forest?

What ways can you encourage people to be safer in forests? What could you tell them?

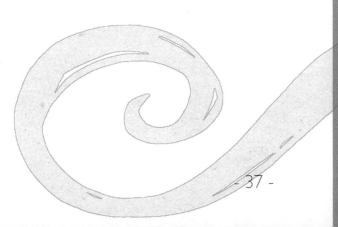

Stock Image

Imagine

Imagine you are in a forest (without fire). What do you see/hear/feel/smell?

What ways can you encourage people to be safer in forests? What do you want to tell them?

If you were going to put up signs in the forest, what would they say?

Learn

Learn how to identify a pine tree. (https://www.playfullearning.net/resource/simple-keys-identifying-conifers-pine-family/)

Find out how to measure the height of a tree. (www.forestry.usu.edu/kids-and-teachers/tree-height)

Make

Make a model of a burned log or tree trunk out of toilet paper rolls. Add animals that would live in and around it.

Draw an oak tree with acorns and animals that might live there.

Resources

Links to all resources can be found at:
www.terrabellabooks.com/s/Links-from-the-book.pdf

Fires

How We Fight Wildfires
www.youtube.com/watch?v=9EzcA3KvEsY

San Francisco Fire Department wooden ladder shop
https://thekidshouldseethis.com/post/the-san-francisco-fire-departments-ladder-shop

Plants & Animals

Woodpeckers
https://www.nationalgeographic.com/animals/article/fires-help-endangered-woodpeckers

California Native Plant Society
https://www.cnps.org/education/students/parents-%20teachers

California Gold

El Dorado County Historical Museum
http://museum.edcgov.us/

Empire Mine State Historic Park
https://www.sierragoldparksfoundation.org/page/empire-mine-state-historic-park/

Forests

Forest Health Workers
www.youtube.com/watch?v=v8ZdldjSk5c

Sounds of the Forest
www.timberfestival.org.uk/soundsoftheforest-soundmap/

Time-lapse video of wildfires in California 1910-2019
www.youtube.com/watch?v=o58Te06fOkw&feature=youtu.be

Native Americans

NAJA Reporting and Indigenous Terminology Guide
https://najanewsroom.com/reporting-guides/

Native People of California
www.kids.nationalgeographic.com/explore/native-americans/native-people-of-california/

Washoe History
https://washoetribe.us

Miwok language
www.native-languages.org/miwok.htm

There is an extensive list of books for students and teachers at:
www.terrabellabooks.com/s/Book-list-for-students

Glossary

adapted – Adjusted to new conditions

backfire – A small fire started on purpose along the edge of a wildfire to burn the fuel out of the path of a fire

brush – An area of shrubs, grasses and other small plants

cavity – A sunken or open area in a tree that usually happens after an injury to the tree

clear-cut – Cut down and remove every tree from an area

climate change – The shift in weather patterns due, at least in part, to human activity, mostly emissions of greenhouse gases

controlled burn – See *prescribed*

cultural burn – Burning practices developed by Indigenous people to renew their ecosystems

disturbance – In ecology, it is a change in the environment resulting in major changes to an ecosystem

duff – Twigs, pine needles, leaves and other fallen parts of plants that are dry or dead

ecological thinning – Removing smaller trees and brush from the forest to restore habitat and reduce wildfires

ecosystem – A community of living things, their physical environment and how they all interact

ember – A hot piece of wood or a coal from a fire that can travel, usually due to wind, and ignite a fire in another area

extinguish – To put out the flame

evacuate – To remove someone from a dangerous place to a safer one

fire break – A strip of open space in a forest to stop the spread of fire

fire line – A barrier to fire made by digging and removing things that can burn

fire scar – An injury to a tree or other plant caused by fire; can be used to determine when a fire occurred

foraging – Searching for food

fuel – A source of energy (in a fire it means anything that can burn)

fungus - Organisms that help the forest absorb nutrients and also help dead wood decompose (they live in many different environments but do need moisture)

giga-fire – Fire that burns more than a million acres

grazing – Eating low-lying grasses and wild vegetation in the outdoors

habitat – The natural, usual or preferred surroundings for living organisms

ignite/ignition – What is needed to start a fire

indigenous – A living thing, or group of things, that are naturally found in a certain area

inhalation – breathing in air or other substances

invasive – Something (plants) stronger than native plants that take over an area

kindling – Small twigs or sticks that are used to start a fire

leached – Passing water over or through a material to remove certain compounds

megafire – A very large, intense wildfire that can be uncontrollable

nutrients – These provide energy for living things

old-growth forest – A forest that has not had much disturbance (also called primary forest)

particles – Very small bits; like dust

polluting – Making something harmful by adding chemical or waste

predators – Animals that hunt other animals

prescribed (burn) – A fire intentionally set to manage a forest

reservation – The Indian reservation system established these tracts of land for Native Americans to live on as white settlers took over their traditional land.

resilience/resilient – Making something stronger so it can survive disturbance and thrive

resin – Produced by many pine trees where it is cut or injured

retardant – Chemicals that are used to slow down or stop a fire from spreading

roost – The place where birds will gather to rest at night

sacred – Something that is respected and has religious purpose

sapling – A very young tree

scales – The thick plate-like parts of a pinecone, which actually hold the seeds

scorched – Burned by fire or heat

shoots – The new growth of a plant as it comes out of the ground

snag – A dead or dying tree that is still standing

species – A group of organisms or living things that have common qualities or characteristics

tamp – To pack or force down firmly

timber – The part of a tree that can be used for building structures; or just trees that are valued for harvesting

traditional burn – The way fire was used by Native American people to keep a forest healthy

vegetation – Plants or a group of plants and the area they cover

water vapor – Water in a gaseous state (fog, steam, mist)

Bibliography

For a complete bibliography go to:
www.terrabellabooks.com/s/Final-Biblio.pdf

Anderson, Kat. Tending the Wild: Native American Knowledge and the Management of California's Natural Resources. Berkeley: University of California Press, 2005.

Bibby, Brian, and Dugan Aguilar. Deeper than Gold: Indian Life in the Sierra Foothills. Berkeley, Calif: Heyday Books, 2005.

Cunningham, Laura. A State of Change: Forgotten Landscapes of California. Berkeley, Calif: Heyday, 2010.

How Fire Shapes Everything | Stephen Pyne, 2016. (www.youtube.com/watch?v=LPC7UQyQQhQ)

Jackson, Louise A. The Sierra Nevada before History: Ancient Landscapes, Early Peoples. Missoula, Mont: Mountain Press Pub. Co, 2010.

Margolin, Malcolm, and California Historical Society, eds. The Way We Lived: California Indian Stories, Songs & Reminiscences. 35th anniversary edition. Berkeley, California: Heyday, California Historical Society, 2017.

Nixon, Guy. A History of the Enduring Washoe People: And Their Neighbors Including the Si Te Cah (Sasquatch). United States: Guy Nixon, 2013.

Noy, Gary, and Rick Heide, eds. The Illuminated Landscape: A Sierra Nevada Anthology. A California Legacy Book. Sierra College Press ; Santa Clara University ; Heyday Books, 2010.

Palley, Stuart. Terra Flamma: Wildfires at Night. Atglen, PA: Schiffer Publishing, Ltd, 2018.

Stewart, Omer Call, Henry T. Lewis, and Kat Anderson. Forgotten Fires: Native Americans and the Transient Wilderness. Norman: University of Oklahoma Press, 2002.

Acknowledgments

Michael and Heather Llewellyn, Llewellyn Studio
Missy Mohler and Ashley Phillips, Sierra Watershed Education Partnerships (SWEP)
Kathy Mick, U.S. Forest Service, Pacific Southwest Region
Darrel Cruz, Washoe Tribe of Nevada and California
Jeff Brown and Faerthen Felix, Sagehen Creek Field Station

Presented to the people of the Truckee-Tahoe region of California, the FOREST ⇌ FIRE project is a partnership between Nevada County Arts Council, Truckee-Donner Recreation and Park District and University of California, Berkeley - Sagehen Creek Field Station, with Educational and Environmental Outreach by Sierra Watershed Education Partnerships. We and FOREST ⇌ FIRE's creators, Llewellyn Studio, are grateful for the support of California Arts Council; California Humanities—a non-profit partner of the National Endowment for the Humanities; Tahoe Truckee Excellence in Education Foundation; Tahoe Truckee Community Foundation, through the Nature Fund and Queen of Hearts Women's Fund; University of Nevada—Reno; Truckee Tahoe Airport District; and many other organizations and individuals.

FOREST ⇌ FIRE

In addition, Nevada County Arts Council and its partners stand in solidarity with all of Nevada County's Indigenous peoples. We acknowledge that our work takes place on the now occupied traditional lands of the Nisenan and Washoe people, who are the past, present and future stewards of this place. We make this first step in our journey to develop relationships and cultural competencies to truly support native sovereignty.

About the Author

PAULA HENSON's great great-grandparents came to California during the Gold Rush but not to search for gold! Paula is an educator who writes children's fiction and non-fiction books relating to the environment, mainly about the importance of water. She is a history-loving, water-conserving former garden designer who has tended gardens (but not forests) in Los Angeles. www.terrabellabooks.com

About the Illustrators

SUE TODD is a professional illustrator of books, magazines, posters and other print material for children and adults. She creates linocut prints with digital color in her yellow studio and gets her best ideas while cycling the nature paths of Toronto. Her art has been commissioned by clients in North America and the UK. In addition to commissioned illustration, she is working on writing and illustrating her own stories for children and playing around with digital portraiture on the iPad. www.suetodd.com

EMILY UNDERWOOD is an artist and educator based in Central California. Blending her background in both science and art, she explores the natural world and its landscape histories through the mediums of painting, printmaking, and bookmaking. She also creates illustrations and interpretive artwork for researching scientists, museums, parks, and other agencies. www.underwoodillustration.com

Made in the USA
Las Vegas, NV
29 March 2025

20220371R10029